HE IS MADE KNIGHT AND HE MOUNTS AND RIDES

And the tale tells how, in a while, one came to him, saying: "Rise, Sir Galwyn, be faithful, fortunate and brave." So he rose up and put on his polished armour and the golden spurs like twin lightnings, and his bright hair was like a sun hidden by the cloudy silver of his plumed helm, and he took up his bright unscarred shield and his stainless long sword and young Sir Galwyn went out therefrom.

His horse was caparisoned in scarlet and cloth of gold and he mounted and rode forth. Trumpets saluted him, and pennons flapped out on a breeze like liquid silver, beneath a golden morning like the first morning of the world, and young Sir Galwyn's charger marched slow and stately with pride, and young Sir Galwyn looked not back whence he had come.

In a while they came to a forest. This was a certain enchanted forest and the trees in this forest were more ancient than any could remember; for it was beneath these trees that, in the olden time, one Sir Morvidus, Earl Warwick, had slain a giant which had assaulted Sir Morvidus with the trunk of a tree torn bodily from the earth; and Sir Morvidus to commemorate this encounter assumed the ragged

MAYDAY

MAYDAY

William Faulkner

INTRODUCTION BY
Carvel Collins

UNIVERSITY OF NOTRE DAME PRESS
NOTRE DAME   LONDON

Library of Congress Cataloging in Publication Data

Faulkner, William, 1897–1962
  Mayday

  I. Title
PS3511.A86M36   813'.5'2   77-376384
ISBN 0-268-01339-X

Manufactured in the United States of America

Contents

v

Introduction

CARVEL COLLINS

To

William Bell Wisdom
(1900–1977)

who not only collected and read
but understood and appreciated

Introduction

William Faulkner wrote, hand-lettered, illustrated, and bound the little book which he titled *Mayday*. He dated it "27 January, 1926," dedicated it to Helen Baird, and gave her the only known copy. Some years later William B. Wisdom acquired it, and not long ago he presented it to the Tulane University Library along with the rest of his Faulkner collection.

The publication of this trade edition seems useful because *Mayday* has not been easily accessible. To preserve the booklet's excellent but fragile condition, Mr. Wisdom understandably wanted to limit the handling of it, but in the early 1950s he generously gave permission for me to make a photocopy in black and white, and in 1962 one in color. He said later that during the years he owned the booklet he had permitted no more than two other scholars to look at it because of what he called "poor judgment" by one of them. Increasingly disturbed by what he considered an unscholarly element of politics in the study of Faulkner—which he compared unfavorably on that score to the study of Thomas Wolfe, about which he was also expert—he continued to limit the availability of *Mayday* and the rest of his Faulkner materials until he turned them over to Tulane and the imaginative, highly professional stewardship of Mrs. Ann S. Gwyn, Head of the Tulane Library's Special Collections Division. Then those who were especially interested were permitted to read *Mayday*. After 1976, when it was one of the features of the excellent public show of the William B. Wisdom Collection of William Faulkner which Mrs. Gwyn arranged at Tulane, the booklet was made quite accessible to serious scholars who could go to New Orleans. In 1977 it became somewhat more available when, with the permission of Mrs. Jill Faulkner Summers, of Mr. Wisdom, and of Mrs. Gwyn, the University of Notre Dame Press published a first-edition facsimile limited to twenty-five presentation copies and one hundred and twenty-five numbered copies. The cost of producing that accurate facsimile in color required selling it at a rather high price, and the dramatic rise in the figure at which that edition is resold in the rare book market has continued to limit its use by readers. Now with the publication of this trade edition the work is at last generally available.

That seems good because *Mayday* is not just a physically attractive piece of marginalia in the life of a Nobel laureate. It has seemed to me ever since Mr. Wisdom in the early 1950s let me read it for the first

4

time to be a valuable aid in revising some of the firmly established misconceptions of Faulkner's art; and it is unique among Faulkner's hand-lettered booklets for directly and significantly bearing on one of his most important works, *The Sound and the Fury*, and through that novel on more of his major writing.

Faulkner produced several hand-lettered booklets in the 1920s, of which I have seen eight copies and have been told of others lost long ago. Of the lost, three were somewhat identified, but the remainder were only vaguely mentioned. The eight copies which it has been possible to inspect are of five titles: A 1920 booklet of poems Faulkner gave to his friend Phil Stone and called *The Lilacs*. A 1920 play called *Marionettes* which survives in a few copies, of which it has been possible to inspect only four. Two 1926 gifts to Helen Baird, one of them *Mayday* and the other an interesting group of sixteen poems titled *Helen: A Courtship*. And *Royal Street*, also of 1926, dedicated to Estelle Oldham Franklin and containing short prose pieces, all but one of which Faulkner previously had published. *Royal Street*, like *Helen: A Courtship*, is not illustrated, but like *Mayday* it does contain several colored initial capital letters. The three lost hand-lettered booklets which Faulkner's acquaintances have been able to describe are all said to have contained poems: one a gift to a man in Memphis, one sold by Faulkner for fifteen dollars to a fellow-student at the University of Mississippi, and one—about which more detail was recollected—a gift from Faulkner to another fellow-student, a girl to whom he sometimes read his poems and showed his drawings. She recalled that soon after she told him she would like to own some of his work, Faulkner made for her a booklet consisting of between five and eight poems and a one-page dramatic dialogue in prose. She remembered that for each of the works in that booklet—which disappeared when a house burned—Faulkner sketched an illustration in black ink and that his illustration for a poem titled "The Asphodel" or "The Asphodels" was an attenuated female figure growing like a plant from a vase or flowerpot. In addition to those three lost hand-lettered booklets were some which Phil Stone said Faulkner had given him from time to time as presents on birthdays and other occasions, all completely disappeared after fire also destroyed Stone's house.

The attractive one-act play, *Marionettes*, was the first of Faulkner's hand-lettered booklets to become generally available. A limited first edition of it was published in 1975 by the University Press of Virginia. Then the Yoknapatawpha Press at Oxford, Mississippi, published a remarkably exact limited facsimile. More recently the University Press of Virginia published a trade edition. In 1950 William Faulkner's mother told me of her amused astonishment when she heard that a copy of *Marionettes*, of which her son in 1920 had sold a few copies for very little and given away others, was being offered in New York for more than a hundred dollars. Had she been alive in 1975, she presumably would have felt greater astonishment, because that year a copy of *Marionettes* sold for $34,000. At least I know that I was startled, for the late owner of that copy had generously mailed it to me rather casually on two occasions some years before—once so that I might compare it with another copy of *Marionettes* which I then owned.

Other authors produced somewhat similar booklets in the period just before and during the early years of Faulkner's career—James Joyce, for example, making one or more. When we remember Faulkner's serious interest in drawing and painting as well as writing and his lack both of money for gifts and of enough outlets for publishing, it seems quite natural that he should have produced these booklets, which incidentally were in some accord with the still sizable arts and crafts activity of the period.

Mayday, besides being the hand-lettered booklet most closely related to Faulkner's major work, is, to the best of my knowledge, unique in an additional, though minor, way. Some of the other booklets, as pointed out above, contain black-ink drawings by Faulkner, for example those which appear effectively throughout *Marionettes*, but the three full-page watercolors in *Mayday* make it the only known Faulkner booklet surviving in good condition which contains colored illustrations. Some years ago I saw another hand-lettered booklet by Faulkner which was illustrated in color—*The Lilacs*, mentioned above as a present from Faulkner to Phil Stone. It had been in Stone's Oxford house which fire destroyed early in the 1940s. Having begun in 1948 his generous and prolonged effort to help me try to understand more about Faulkner's fiction, Stone in the early 1950s gave permission to go through the debris of his former house in hope of finding some remnant of Faulkner's apprentice writings. After Mrs. Stone and I had taken from the site of the fire, which had leveled the house almost ten years earlier, a number of damp, charred lumps, bundles, and stray sheets of paper and I had separated and spread them in the Stones' back yard to dry, a badly burned booklet appeared among what turned out to be more than four hundred and seventy pages of Faulkner's early writing. Containing at least nine poems, the booklet is hand-lettered and bound by Faulkner, signed by him, titled *The Lilacs*, and dated January 1, 1920. A charred fragment of the sheet opposite the first page of text shows that it is a colored illustration, but the full content of that little painting is forever lost.

Drawing and painting had attracted William Faulkner from his childhood years. In his determination to be an artist of some sort, he early considered a possible career in graphic arts as well as writing. His mother told me that when very young he had shown an interest in drawing and a talent for it. She cited among other proofs a sketch he had made as a child when the town of Oxford had begun to use a new tank wagon for sprinkling the streets. He had come home excited from watching the operation of that more sophisticated equipment and eager to describe it to his family. When he realized that his description was inadequate he quickly drew a picture of the wagon with its valves and sprinklers, so detailed as to astonish his mother. She did go on to say, however, that because his chief interest turned out to be writing, she felt she may have pushed him too hard toward drawing and painting in his early years.

Faulkner apparently submitted a drawing to a national magazine when he was fourteen. He drew several high school cartoons which a former classmate of his, Mrs. Frederick V. B. Demarest, preserved and kindly permitted to be photocopied a quarter-century ago. A drawing for the 1917 University of Mississippi annual is his first known published work of any kind. He made a couple of sketches during the next year in letters from New Haven, Connecticut; later in that year of 1918, while in Canada for R.A.F. training, he made several sketches in class notebooks and more than a dozen in letters from Toronto. In University of Mississippi annuals between 1917 and 1922, as in a humor magazine at the University in 1925, surely the outstanding drawings are those which he contributed. In 1921 during the several weeks he spent in a second and rather poignant sojourn at New Haven which apparently is unknown to his biographers, Faulkner was writing seriously and trying to place what he wrote with publishers, but he also was trying seriously to improve his graphic skill, especially with pencil and colored crayon. In the shorter time he spent at New York City the same year, he reported that he planned to enter a night art class in order in learn more about line and that his boss in the book department at Lord & Taylor felt it would be easy for him to sell his drawings. Faulkner explained that he hoped to earn money by drawing, possibly advertisements, while trying to establish himself as a writer.

There was in the attic of his mother's house a black, metal artist box lettered with his name and, to judge by what his mother told me, possibly acquired well along in his life. And through later years he would make skillful drawings, as in several of his letters. But by 1926 when he illustrated *Mayday* with watercolors and sketches, he was no longer expecting to give his professional artistic life to drawing and painting. *Helen: A Courtship*, his gift to Helen Baird in the same year he gave her *Mayday*, contains a poem titled "Bill," in which he said of himself that "first and last/His heart's whole dream" had been "With space and light to feed it through his eyes,/ But with the gift of tongues he was accursed." He had stated that fact more gently in a 1925 newspaper piece,

"Out of Nazareth," writing that his New Orleans friend Spratling's "hand has been shaped to a brush as mine has (alas!) not" and adding that "words are my meat and bread and drink." From then on his drawing and painting would be intended only for private consumption—for his family and friends and, in *Mayday*, for Helen Baird.

Faulkner met her at New Orleans in 1925 and quickly fell in love. She told me in 1954 and 1962 that he had proposed marriage. Refusing his proposal, she had married Guy Lyman in 1927. This was Faulkner's second experience of having a woman he asked to marry him decide to marry another: In 1918 he and Estelle Oldham of Oxford had planned a wedding. One of their close friends in that period, to whom Faulkner was to give a copy of *Marionettes* as a 1920 Christmas present, told me they had taken out a marriage license. But parental and other pressures ended their plan, and Estelle Oldham married Cornell Franklin. She and Faulkner eventually would marry—in 1929, after her divorce—but while Faulkner was unsuccessfully courting Helen Baird in 1925 and 1926 at New Orleans and on the Mississippi Gulf Coast, Estelle was with her first husband in the Orient.

Introduction

That Faulkner then was intensely in love with Helen Baird seems clearly demonstrated by his later letters to her, by what three of their friends and one of her relatives have recalled, and—of most literary interest—by his recollections of her and of his feeling for her which he worked into his fiction.

He was to put some of his experience of frustrated love for Helen Baird into his presentation of the girl Patricia in his second novel, *Mosquitoes*, which, like *Mayday*, he dedicated to Helen. Though Faulkner briefly inserted himself into that novel under his own name as a character who is a writer, he also put himself into the novel's young crewman who hopelessly adores Patricia and goes with her on the swamp journey among the mosquitoes. To the crewman Faulkner gave the name "David," which more than once in his fiction he applied to a psychologically autobiographical character. But it is in *The Wild Palms*, published 1939, that Faulkner drew most meaningfully on his love for Helen Baird. In the years after he wrote *Mayday*, Faulkner spent time now and then with her and her husband Guy. This association enlarged the feeling he had begun to have in 1925, which, joined with the effects of other experiences, helped give to *The Wild Palms* the poignance that has contributed to its remarkable rise in critical evaluation. Faulkner set the novel's final scenes of Charlotte Rittenmeyer and Harry Wilbourne in the Mississippi Gulf Coast town of Pascagoula, where he had known Helen in the mid-1920s. Though Helen Baird Lyman, of course, never abandoned her husband and children nor was she involved in any association like Charlotte's with Harry, Faulkner did give Charlotte some of the physical characteristics of the Helen he had loved, as well as her artistic activities, her intensity, and the compelling attraction she had had for him. He once said that he thought of Helen as a "flame," and in Charlotte Rittenmeyer, I think, he created a person who is trying to live by Walter Pater's famous admonition. Most criticism of *The Wild Palms* has considered Charlotte quite reprehensible, a judgment which should be reexamined, though this is not the place to pursue it in the necessary detail.

In 1963 Mrs. Meta Wilde kindly began to give the invaluable help of recalling in detail her association with William Faulkner, allowing me to read her many letters from him, and generously answering biographical questions. Her recollections and Faulkner's letters to her make clear that though much of the intensity of Harry Wilbourne's feeling at the end of *The Wild Palms* surely comes from the situation in which Faulkner found himself because of his great and hopeless attraction to Meta, Faulkner had a great part of the novel in mind before he met Meta and in writing it was also drawing on recollections of his frustrated earlier love for Helen. In doing so he had come a great distance: In 1939 in *The Wild Palms* Harry Wilbourne's rejection of suicide because of his loving and admiring determination to keep alive the memory of Charlotte is a world away from Sir Galwyn's disillusionment about love and his suicide, which Faulkner in 1926 featured in *Mayday* with an irony that owes much to James Branch Cabell.

Most readers who have lived several decades will recognize at once the indebtedness of *Mayday* to Cabell's fiction. At the time Faulkner was preparing *Mayday* as a gift to Helen Baird, Cabell's reputation was at its height. In 1925 Carl Van Doren had said that "Cabell is already a classic if any American novelist of this century is." Benjamin de Casseres had called Cabell the "Prometheus of an American Renaissance." Faulkner's sophisticated New Orleans friend, John McClure, who had a significant and so-far unrecorded influence on Faulkner, had written in 1925 on the justly famous book page he edited for the *Times-Picayune* that "Mr. Cabell is one of perhaps a dozen men of our time . . . almost certain to be recognized by posterity." Then Cabell's reputation quickly dropped. By 1928 even John McClure wrote that he "had his rise and is having his fall. The seeds of corruption in his earlier works have grown to weeds." But when Faulkner was producing *Mayday*, Cabell's high reputation seemed secure.

Into *The Line of Love*, first published in 1905 and revised in 1921, Cabell put what was to be a major theme of much of his best-known work: Ideal love can never be sustained; every idealized love is lost, whether the lover wins or loses the beloved. Hardly a new idea, witness as a sample—and putting aside not only the literature of antiquity but first-rate later poetry—these lines from Emerson's "Each and All":

At last she came to his hermitage,
Like the bird from the woodlands to the cage;—
The gay enchantment was undone,
A gentle wife, but fairy none.

For several years Cabell energetically gave this view much of his attention. Edmund Wilson, in attempts during the 1950s to revive Cabell's reputation, praised certain works but spoke disparagingly about the "theme in Cabell's writings which I have always found it most difficult to sympathize with . . . that of his persistent nostalgia for the ideal beautiful women of his adolescent imaginings."

But to rework in *Mayday* Cabell's best-known theme must have been psychologically useful to Faulkner at the start of 1926 because of his troubled relationship with Helen Baird: he was more attracted to her than she to him, and he was finding that frustration painful. Mrs. Margery Gumbel told me that in New Orleans the year before Faulkner produced *Mayday* he had talked with her about Helen Baird's lack of response to his courtship. And Helen's aunt, the late Mrs. Edward Martin, recalled that in 1926 while Faulkner was writing *Mosquitoes* in a cottage next door to her own Pascagoula beach house, he had told her dramatically and passionately how he felt about the absent Helen.

Some years before, between 1919 and 1922, Faulkner had fallen in love with a young woman at Charleston, Mississippi, where he often went to visit Phil Stone while Stone was working there in one of his family's law offices. When she did not respond to

Faulkner's affection he felt considerable emotional distress. But he cured himself, he told Stone, by deliberately developing mental pictures of that otherwise idealized person engaged in the least romantic regularly repeated acts of our species. On a higher level he may have been making a somewhat similar attempt to exorcise the pain of his unsuccessful suit for Helen Baird's affection by adopting in *Mayday* Cabell's theme and ironic manner. The fact that the booklet which he gave to Helen later in 1926 than his gift of *Mayday* was titled *Helen: A Courtship* might suggest at first glance that *Mayday* was not the product of real hopelessness about their relationship; but most of the poems in *Helen: A Courtship* had been written before he wrote *Mayday*—and many of them speak sadly of love unreturned. The courtship in the title of that booklet he seems already to have recognized as unsuccessful.

Most of Cabell's *Line of Love*, like *Mayday*, is presented as the repetition of a "tale" previously told, with much of the tale, like all of *Mayday*, set in the Middle Ages. The action of *Line of Love* begins "on Walburga's Eve, on the day that ends April" and moves at once to a first day of May which, like Faulkner's *Mayday*, has tragic elements not traditionally part of that "day of new beginnings": In *Line of Love* when a song performed on May Day mentions death as well as love, a young man calls it a "very foolish and pessimistical old song." Then the young man learns that time has passed, but he magically has remained young while the girl he had expected thirty years before to marry has become "an imposing matron in middle life." When he asks whether she is indeed his Adelaide, she replies, "Yes, every pound of me, poor boy, and that says much." When he chides her for infidelity because she married another while he was under enchantment, she reasonably points out that if they had stayed together she would "be just as I am to-day, and you would be tied to me." Then the man, still young and still romantic, falls in love with his former fiancée's daughter and, having learned nothing, feels sure that this is "a love which would endure unchanged as long as his life lasted." The tale of this young bride and her groom ends with a motif Cabell repeated continually in *Line of Love* and was to use in later books: After the man and woman marry, romance fades, but he "made her, they relate, a fair husband, as husbands go." One of the characters in *The Dain Curse* by Faulkner's friend Dashiell Hammett calls

Cabell "a romanticist in the same sense that the wooden horse was Trojan."

Subsequent segments of *Line of Love* present variations on the theme of disillusionment which Faulkner repeated in *Mayday*, but Cabell ended this book and others in a less pessimistic way than the way Faulkner—for reasons to be discussed later—ended *Mayday:* Cabell's protagonists here and in later novels come to accept life's reality, but Faulkner's Sir Galwyn kills himself. When Cabell ended *Line of Love* by suggesting the possibility "that to live unbefooled by love is at best a shuffling and debt-dodging business" and that "this unreasoned, transitory surrender" may "be the most high and, indeed, the one requisite action which living affords," he was approaching the position Faulkner would take in *The Wild Palms* of 1939 but did not take in *Mayday* of the mid-1920s. In *Mayday* Faulkner drew even more obviously from some of Cabell's subsequently published ironic allegories, but it seems possible that he read *Line of Love*, and he even may have lifted from it a name which he put into *Mayday*.

Cabell's *The Cream of the Jest*—first published in 1917, revised in 1922, and among his best-known novels—contains an element which bears on one of the major elements of *Mayday:* Kennaston, Cabell's twentieth-century protagonist who lives much in dreams where his beloved ideal woman is the unattainable Ettarre, at the end of the novel is simultaneously elated and terrified when Ettarre's hands reach toward him and "the universe seemed to fold about him," and he thinks that possibly it is as death that Ettarre is coming to him in that final dream. But, unlike Sir Galwyn of *Mayday*, who finally does join Death in the river, Kennaston does not join Ettarre, instead settling down somewhat contentedly with his wife of reality. Other elements of *Mayday* appear in *The Cream of the Jest*, but a more obvious source for all of them is Cabell's *Jurgen*, which, incidentally, Faulkner had cited directly in his first novel, completed the year before he completed *Mayday*.

Made especially famous by a publicized censorship trial which ended in 1922, *Jurgen* was the best-known of Cabell's novels. Many elements of *Jurgen* and of *Mayday* are alike: the settings, the sardonic ironies, the joking anachronisms, that each protagonist is "nothing" except a "shadow," that lives are possibly only dreams, the protagonists' loves of even legendary women (Guenevere for Jurgen, Yseult for Sir Galwyn) which bring only

sighs of boredom when the women are no longer
unattainable, the protagonists' uncertainties about
what it really is which they desire, love affairs with
somewhat frighteningly inhuman women (Jurgen's
Lady of the Lake, connected somehow with the
moon and mistress of a ship handled by a mouse- and
bat-like crew, and Sir Galwyn's Princess Aelia, connected somehow with the morning star and driver of
a chariot drawn by dolphins), meaningful dis-
cussions about time with immortal personifications
who envy the protagonists their mortal ability to feel
important, women inopportunely concerned with
the condition of their hair, the return at the end of
each book to the place of beginning where Jurgen and
Sir Galwyn have brief recapitulatory final meetings
with women they have known, and the similarity of
the opening phrases of the two books as well as the
complete identity of their closing sentences: "Thus it
was in the old days."

Mayday does not contain the somewhat leer-
ing pornographic element of *Jurgen*, the continual
references to the protagonist's penetrating lance, for
example; but of much more significance is the dif-
ference between the conclusions of the two works.
Cabell in *Jurgen*, as in *The Cream of the Jest* and

elsewhere in his fiction, ended with a somewhat optimistic resolution of the protagonist's problem. Jurgen, after his year of moving through many regions and love affairs while wearing his magically youthful body, becomes again the middle-aged man he was at the beginning, but he is changed by his adventures in one important way: disillusioned about idealized romantic love as well as about continually emphasized sensuality, he is at last willing to settle down with his wife of ten years in the realization that they have much in common. But Faulkner in *Mayday* let Sir Galwyn find no such optimistic compromise, sending him instead into the river.

Sir Galwyn's suicide, like certain other elements not shared with Cabell's novels, is surely there because of the connection between *Mayday* and Faulkner's first major work, *The Sound and the Fury*. It seems likely that in writing *Mayday* Faulkner was not only making a gift for Helen Baird, but—artist at all times—was giving himself an opportunity to write a small triangulatory piece of fiction related to the early phases of his creating *The Sound and the Fury*. The commonly held and sometimes emotionally maintained opinion is that Faulkner did not begin writing *The Sound and the Fury* until 1928 or, at the earliest, 1927—too late for it to be connected in this way with *Mayday* of 1926. But there is contrary evidence, previously unavailable. Not much about Faulkner's 1925 months at Paris is known to his biographers except the information in a notably inaccurate memoir by the late William Spratling and the few Paris letters by Faulkner which have been published from among those which survive, but a man with whom Faulkner became friendly in Paris met him often for meals and long walks about the city. If that friend came to pick up Faulkner at his hotel room—first in the Rue Jacob and later in Servandoni—and Faulkner was not there, the friend while waiting for him would read with his permission whatever Faulkner had been writing. He told me that one of Faulkner's works in progress which he read then was about a girl and her brothers and became *The Sound and the Fury*. I thought perhaps his memory—always excellent about everything we discussed which could be checked—had stumbled here and that what he had read was part of Faulkner's unfinished attempt to write in 1925 a novel about Elmer Hodge, which I had first seen in the 1950s as a guest of Faulkner's editor, Saxe Commins, who took it briefly out of a box of many manuscripts Faulkner had just brought from Mississippi to Commins' house in Princeton. But Faulkner's friend dismissed my question, saying that he had read nothing whatever about an Elmer or any family such as the Hodges I described for him in detail and adding that what he had seen at Faulkner's Paris room in 1925 came clearly to his mind again when he read *The Sound and the Fury* after its publication four years later. Earlier he had told me that on their walks, one of them in the Forest of Meudon, Faulkner spoke of two families he intended to write about. One family started out poor and moved continually, with children leaving until only the youngest boy remained. The father finally struck oil and the son tried to become a painter. The other family, formerly well-to-do, had a daughter who got in trouble and left home, a mentally defective son, a son who committed suicide, and one who was "a sharper." Obviously the first family is that of the *Elmer* manuscripts while the second is that of *The Sound and the Fury*.

Presumably everyone needs to work hard to avoid naiveté about when and how artists "begin" their creations. Bernard DeVoto used to remark that a novelist should wear twenty-four hours a day a placard saying "Author at work," and it is possible, for example, to make a small argument that Faulkner "began" *A Fable* (1954) at New Haven in 1918 while listening to William Aspenwall Bradley in The Brick Row Book Shop. Certainly there have been naive interpretations of Faulkner's repeated public statement about *how* he began *The Sound and the Fury:* at first as just Benjy's section, thinking that was enough, and then after realizing it was not enough, writing Quentin's section, and then continuing that pattern of uncertainty. Two well-known and highly intelligent critics, believing what Faulkner stated, have said in print that thus we see how haphazard and uncontrolled were Faulkner's practice of composition and the resultant novel. An odd concept in view of the fact that no matter how many uncertain attempts may or may not have preceded the final manuscript that manuscript shows no discontinuity, Benjy's section and the others being magnificently interlocked and integrated, with no hint of the existence of earlier unassimilated chunks. If, however, one takes the enormous risk of believing what Faulkner said in interviews and those published volumes which transcribe his question and answer sessions, such chunks may have existed and what Faulkner's friend read at his Paris room in 1925 may have been one of them. But taking that risk here seems unnecessary.

It is quite obvious that *Mayday* has much in common with Quentin Compson's monologue in *The Sound and the Fury*. Each protagonist, Sir Galwyn and Quentin, has spent in solitary vigil the night preceding the start of his story. Each of the two pieces of fiction begins by showing the arrival of day beyond the protagonist's window. Some of the wording in the opening paragraphs of *Mayday* is similar to wording at the start of Quentin's monologue in Faulkner's holograph of *The Sound and the Fury*, before he revised it into the printed version of 1929. Sir Galwyn and Quentin both have a girl on their minds from the start: for the knight she is one "with long shining hair" who turns out to be sister Death, while for the Mississippian she is his sister Caddy, who is, in a sense, the death of him. Both young men travel restlessly throughout their narratives, though Quentin is certain from the start that his goal is to die when darkness comes, while Sir Galwyn is uncertain about what he is seeking but finds, at the end, that his goal, too, has been death. Quentin thinks about Saint Francis of Assisi, and Sir Galwyn actually speaks with him, twice. Quentin recalls a conversation in which his father tells him that life is meaningless because of the passage of time; Sir Galwyn meets in a wood a strange man whose name is Time and who gives Sir Galwyn the same nihilistic message Mr. Compson gives Quentin. And each of the protagonists drowns himself in a river.

Another, especially interesting, connection of *Mayday* to *The Sound and the Fury* is the similarity between the traveling companions of Sir Galwyn— Hunger and Pain—and the fellow monologists of Quentin Compson—his brothers Benjy and Jason. That connection requires here some background and discussion.

Many readers of Faulkner have felt, under the guidance of some of the early critics and their latter-day disciples, that the chief—even the *only*— function of his fiction is to give information about life in Mississippi and the South in general. I was struck not long ago by the persistence of that view when an intelligent university teacher in Michigan told me with enthusiasm of his assigning Faulkner's novels to his students just so they would understand the South. Faulkner obviously did write about Mississippi, commendably basing much of his work on the life he knew well from having been all his life a part of it. So it is quite legitimate to point out at length any regional or historical or topical aspects of his fiction. The only error, it would seem, is to fail to see that his best fiction goes beyond the regional or the topical or the historical and that if it did not do so, we would not be reading it today. During World War II, when Camus and his associates in the French underground turned with excitement to Faulkner's fiction and laid down much of the foundation for the growing interest in his work which led to his Nobel Prize and present wide acceptance in academia, they surely did not do so because of an interest in learning sociological details about a particular section of a foreign country. They must have felt that Faulkner's works had a more universal application, had something to say to them of more direct and personal import than "regional studies."

Presumably sociology and regional studies recognize that to be valuable they should deal primarily with—or at least identify—the typical. But typicality is a quality notably lacking in the surface stories of many of Faulkner's better novels: In *The Sound and the Fury* we meet instead the Compson family, with the father an alcoholic, the mother a bedridden hypochondriac, the daughter a prostitute, and of the three sons, one an idiot, one a sadist, and one a student at Harvard. In *Absalom, Absalom!* the remarkably untypical Sutpen family. In *Light in August* a major character, the Reverend Hightower, with his dedication—lifelong—to daily observation of an imaginary military horse outfit which creates for him every afternoon in the quiet Jefferson street an astonishing five o'clock rush. Or in *As I Lay Dying* the Bundren family with its hardly typical Mississippi funeral requiring nine days and accompanied by flood, fire, and a flock of buzzards. Faulkner himself said in 1956, ". . . it does sort of amuse me when I hear 'em talking about the sociological picture that I present in something like *As I Lay Dying*, for instance." Much of Faulkner's fiction is about matters other than sociology, and that *Mayday* in a small way points a finger for us in that direction I would like now to argue.

In preparing this hand-lettered gift booklet Faulkner perhaps was primarily saving time by making use of several elements he already had in mind during the early stages of work which went into one of his major novels, *The Sound and the Fury*; but at the same time he also may have been helping on in some way his ultimate creation of that novel: *The Sound and the Fury* is an allegorical work which uses methods Faulkner learned from Joyce's novel *Ulysses*, one of those methods being to make the surface of a story as realistic as any novel by Zola but to place beneath its surface, yet significantly related to the surface, elements of a myth or of a literary work (in *Ulysses* it is *The Odyssey*) or of other patterns (one in *Ulysses* is the chart of human anatomy). Zola could make a section of one of his novels correspond with the Garden of Eden, but—and this is the main point here—he did not maintain in that section the surface realism of the rest of the novel, which is quite different from what Joyce did as a main feature of *Ulysses*. This aspect of Joyce's work is allegory of a new kind, quite unlike the overt allegory of, say, *Pilgrim's Progress*. Joyce's Leopold Bloom is a totally realistic resident of 1904 Dublin while at the same time a figure constantly to be compared and contrasted with Homer's Ulysses—quite different from Bunyan's openly allegorical "Mr. Honest," "Mr. Cruelty," or "Mr. Legality." In *The Sound and the Fury* Faulkner wrote a Joycean allegory which shows a realistic surface but has much going on symbolically beneath it, whereas in *Mayday* he wrote a Bunyanesque allegory. One of

31

the major values of *Mayday* is that, as a piece related to the much more important novel and as an allegory of the older type with no necessity to be realistic, it shows Faulkner's interest in allegory and plainly displays some of the significant elements which in *The Sound and the Fury* lie below the surface.

Their plain display in *Mayday* gives support to an opinion about part of Faulkner's structure in *The Sound and the Fury* which I have been trying to promote since 1952—with considerable objection by some of Faulkner's early critics and their epigones. At the 1952 meeting of The English Institute, in a paper titled "The Interior Monologues of *The Sound and the Fury*," I described Faulkner's conscious use in that novel of Freudian concepts which had become well-known in the 1920s when the new psychology had burst upon the postwar literary world. That paper was published in *English Institute Essays, 1952* and has been fully reprinted since in Irving Malin's collection *Psychoanalysis and American Fiction* (1965) and James B. Meriwether's collection *The Merrill Studies in The Sound and the Fury* (1970), and in shortened form in two other collections. So here I will take only the space necessary to suggest its connection with *Mayday*.

Introduction

Quantities of evidence within *The Sound and the Fury* make clear that for the character of Benjy Compson, Faulkner systematically drew on Freud's description of what Freud called the "Id"; for Quentin Compson, he drew on Freud's description of the "Ego"; and for their brother Jason Compson, on Freud's description of the "Superego." Using techniques demonstrated by Joyce in *Ulysses*, Faulkner skillfully made the three brothers "real" characters in the novel, while simultaneously letting them embody those three abstractions in great detail. The class of critics committed over the years to believing that the chief or only value of Faulkner's fiction is its depiction of life in a particular region of the United States and that to show interest in its various philosophical and psychological aspects is wrong have made the term "reductive" a cliché of their objections. Actually, one can claim with reason that just the opposite is true, that to point out how many things Faulkner successfully could do at once in a novel only helps readers get more for their money.

The Sound and the Fury consists of four parts, in the first three of which each of the Compson brothers presents a long monologue. The order in which they perform—Benjy, then Quentin, then

Jason—is the order in which Freud stated that the three parts of the human personality develop: first the Id, then the Ego, and finally the Super-ego. If we visualize the three monologists as speaking to us from a stage, we are aware that Quentin is in the middle, with Benjy on his right hand and Jason on his left hand. Faulkner placed Sir Galwyn of *Mayday* in the same position, for the young knight finds that he is accompanied by "a small green design with a hundred prehensile mouths which stood at his right hand, and the small green design was called Hunger" and by "a small red design with a hundred restless hands, which stood at his left hand, and the small red design was called Pain." These two bluntly allegorical figures—which appear in all but one of Faulkner's illustrations—pull and haul Sir Galwyn throughout *Mayday*. Faulkner's final illustration of the booklet is the drawing in which Sir Galwyn stands behind his gravestone with the smooth-topped figure of Hunger on his right and the jagged-topped figure of Pain on his left. Hunger is an aspect of the Freudian Id which Faulkner emphasized during his characterization of Benjy Compson in *The Sound and the Fury*—hunger for pleasure-giving affection, from his sister Caddy. An aspect of the Super-ego which Faulkner emphasized in Jason Compson is Jason's censorious objection to that sister and the extent to which his objection leads him to inflict pain. Quentin Compson, like his brother Benjy, hungers for Caddy, and he also punishes himself for that hungering in the painful way of his brother Jason, in fact giving himself the supreme punishment of death. The two styles of Quentin's monologue support this division within himself, because when he is hungering for Caddy his monologue moves closer to the style of Benjy's monologue and when he is painfully making arrangements to kill himself his style moves closer to that of Jason's monologue. Thus an aspect of the Freudian Ego which Faulkner consciously emphasized in Quentin is the condition of being in the middle as mediator between the hungering Id and the painfully punishing Super-ego, a position which Quentin is too weak to maintain, so he drowns himself—with Faulkner thus continuing to parallel Freud, who had stated that if the hungering from the Id is strong and the painfully opposing pressure from the Super-ego is overly harsh, a weak Ego, in the middle, will be destroyed.

In addition to drawing on Freud's theories about the structure of human personality, Faulkner seems to have used somewhat more philosophical speculations originally published by Freud in 1920 and published in English in 1922 and 1924: *Mayday* and *The Sound and the Fury* both feature the close association between the instinct Freud named "Eros" and the death instinct Freud never formally named but which soon was called "Thanatos" by others, including some of the literary acquaintances Faulkner had made in New Orleans the year before he wrote *Mayday* for Helen Baird.

Having said this, one should point out that to report Faulkner's conscious use of the writings of Freud does not make that report, as it has been called, a "Freudian" treatment of Faulkner or his fiction. All the ideas of Freud which Faulkner elaborately used while creating *The Sound and the Fury* were quite available to him in print in English, and his use of them was deliberate—and in reporting that fact one is no more "Freudian" than one is "Shakespearean" in reporting that Faulkner also consciously based some of the structure of *The Sound and the Fury* on *Macbeth*. I might point out that though what Faulkner thought of these interpretations cannot be positively stated, he did read them, and when aspects of them came up in our conversations he courteously avoided making any objections. In fact, among other supportive actions, he took one which was especially surprising but suggested that he had not been displeased by this general critical approach to his work. On October 12, 1955, the Director of Chatto & Windus, Ltd., sent me from London a letter which began:

Dear Mr. Collins,
    I am writing at the suggestion of William Faulkner, who tells me that you are writing a critical book on his work. As you may know, my firm has published Mr. Faulkner for many years, and if you have not already made arrangements with an English publisher for your book, we should very much like an opportunity of seeing it when it is done.

Though that letter does not prove Faulkner agreed with the view of *The Sound and the Fury* summarized so briefly here, it does suggest that he was willing to volunteer support toward making more publicly available this kind of criticism about his work. When Mr. Wisdom generously permitted an early examination of *Mayday*, it too seemed to me supportive because it clearly demonstrates in a small but overt way Faulkner's "allegorical" turn of mind and gives significant aid to the argument that in *The Sound and the Fury* Quentin Compson is a central figure of a drama which is more philosophical and psychological than sociological.

In conclusion it seems well to note that Faulkner's titles for his fiction usually are an effective part of his works and that the title of this hand-lettered booklet is no exception. The drowning of Sir Galwyn at the end of *Mayday* makes the title especially fitting. Although Faulkner was interested in the affirmative aspects of the first day of May—witness his inscribing the date as "Mayday 1951" or perhaps, because of the difficulties of his handwriting, as "May day 1951" in a book he gave to Joan Williams at Bard College—in his fiction he employed May Day pessimistically, using that traditionally optimistic time of new beginnings in sardonic contrast with fictional disasters then taking place. For example, he originally expected to use *Mayday* as the title for his first novel, *Soldiers' Pay*, which he finished in mid-1925 and in which the conventionally hopeful change of April into May is accompanied by the aviator protagonist's death from combat injury. (It is well to remember that Faulkner, with his interest in aviation, surely knew about the voice signal of distress, the French *"m'aidez"* which had become "mayday" for speakers of English.) Into *The Wild Palms* Faulkner would write contrasts between tragic events and the optimistic expectations traditional to early May. And for this 1926 hand-lettered booklet, so closely related to the most poignant monologue of *The Sound and the Fury* and prepared as a gift for a young woman who had refused to marry him, Faulkner selected a title which left no doubt that he was giving to one of May Day's happy traditions an explicit twist toward sorrow: Faulkner's acquaintance, the late folklorist Arthur Palmer Hudson, collected in Mississippi several examples of the popular belief that a young person looking into the water of a stream on May Day will see there the face of the one he or she will marry. At the start of *Mayday* Sir Galwyn has a vision which shows to him in "hurrying dark waters . . . a face all young and red and white, and with long shining hair." At the end of the story, after a number of adventures, Sir Galwyn comes to the stream of that initial vision. When he again sees there the face of the same girl, he joins her in the water—while Saint Francis identifies her as "Little sister Death." Eliot's "The Waste Land" says that April is the cruelest month; Faulkner's title here suggests May first can be the cruelest day.

A NOTE ON THIS EDITION

The limited first edition of *Mayday*, published in 1977 by the University of Notre Dame Press, reproduced in facsimile the original's hand lettering, colored capital initials, and three watercolor illustrations. It also matched the original booklet's page size of approximately 5 by 6½ inches.

This trade edition omits the colored capital letters and one small decorative page number and sets the text in type. With the exception of substituting "arguing" for "arguring" on page 65, it follows Faulkner's original spelling, capitalization, and punctuation even when they are inconsistent or incorrect. Because Faulkner's hand-lettering does not differentiate between *u* and *v* or *g* and *q* it sometimes has been necessary to estimate what spelling he intended. Faulkner's hand-lettered reversals of *s*, *S*, *N*, and *J* have also been normalized here in the type.

Introduction

Although this edition uses Faulkner's running heads and thus has the same number of pages as the original, the length of the pages has been made uniform, with the result that the portion of the text which appears on each page differs somewhat from that on the equivalent page in the original.

Faulkner's two black and white illustrations are the endsheets in the original booklet. His three watercolor illustrations, separated in the original, are together in this edition, their placement indicated by captions.

MAYDAY

by

WILLIAM FAULKNER

to thee

O wise and lovely

this:

a fumbling in darkness

Oxford, Mississippi, 27 January, 1926.

nd the tale tells how at last one came to him. Dawn had already come without, flushing up the high small window so that this high small window which had been throughout the night only a frame for slow and scornful stars became now as a rose unfolding on the dark wall of the chapel. The song of birds came up on the dawn, and the young spring waking freshly, golden and white and troubling: flowers were birdcries about meadows unseen and birdcries were flowers necklaced about the trees. Then the sun like a swordblade touched his own stainless long sword, his morion and hauberk and greaves, and his spurs like twin golden light-nings where they rested beneath the calm sorrowful gaze of the Young Compassionate One, touching his own young face where he had knelt all night on a stone floor, waiting for day.

And it was as though he had passed through a valley between shelving vague hills where the air was gray and smelled of spring, and had come at last upon a dark hurrying stream which, as he watched, became filled suddenly with atoms of color like dart-ing small fish, and the water was no longer dark.

"What does this signify?" he asked of a small green design with a hundred prehensile mouths which stood at his right hand, and the small green design was called Hunger.

"Wait," replied Hunger. And the darting small fish began to coalesce and to assume familiar forms. First the dark ones segregated and the light ones segregated and became stabilized and began to follow each other in measured regular succession.

"What does this signify?" he asked of a small red design with a hundred restless hands, which stood at his left hand, and the small red design was called Pain.

48

"Wait," replied Pain. And in the water there appeared a face which was vaguely familiar, as the green design on his right hand and the red design at his left were familiar, and then other faces; and he leaned nearer above the waters and Hunger and Pain drew closer and he knew that he was not ever to lose them. The stream was now like an endless tapestry unfolding before him. All the faces he had known and loved and hated were there, impersonal now and dispassionate; and familiar places—cottages and castles, battlements and walled towers; and forests and meads, all familiar but small, much smaller than he had remembered.

"What does this signify?" he repeated, and Hunger and Pain drew subtly nearer and said together:

"Wait."

The tapestry unrolled endlessly. It now seemed on the point of assuming a definite pattern, what he did not know, but Hunger and Pain drew subtly nearer. Here was now in the dark hurrying water a stark thin face more beautiful than death, and it was Fortitude; and a tall bright one like a pillar of silver fire, and this one was Ambition; and knights in

49

gold and silver armour and armour of steel, bearing lances with scarlet pennons passed remote and slow and majestic as clouds across a sunset that was as blown trumpets at evening. Himself appeared at last, tiny in mock battle with quarter staff and blunt lance and sword, and Hunger lay in his belly like fire and Pain lay in all his limbs. Then Hunger touched him and said Look! and there in the hurrying dark waters was a face all young and red and white, and with long shining hair like a column of fair sunny water; and he thought of young hyacinths in the spring, and honey and sunlight. He looked upon the face for a long while, and the hundred prehensile mouths of Hunger and the hundred restless hands of Pain were upon him.

Near the stream was a tree covered with bright never-still leaves of a thousand unimaginable colors, and the tree spoke and when the tree spoke the leaves whirled into the air and spun about it. The tree was an old man with a long shining beard like a silver cuirass and the leaves were birds of a thousand kinds and colors. And he replied to the tree, saying: "What sayest thou, good Saint Francis?"

But the good Saint Francis answered only: "Wait, it is not yet time."

Then Pain touched him and he looked again into the waters. The face in the waters was the face of a girl, and Pain and Hunger lay in all his limbs and body so that he burned like fire. And the girl in the dark hurrying stream raised her white arms to him and he would have gone to her, but Pain drew him one way and Hunger drew him another way so that he could not move as she sank away from him into the dark stream that was filled with darting frag-ments of sound and color. Soon these too became indistinct and then the water was once more opaque and silent and hurrying, filling the world about him until he was as one kneeling on a stone floor in a dark place, waiting for day.

And the tale tells how, in a while, one came to him, saying: "Rise, Sir Galwyn, be faithful, for-tunate and brave." So he rose up and put on his polished armour and the golden spurs like twin lightnings, and his bright hair was like a sun hidden by the cloudy silver of his plumed helm, and he took up his bright unscarred shield and his stainless long sword and young Sir Galwyn went out therefrom.

His horse was caparisoned in scarlet and cloth of gold and he mounted and rode forth. Trumpets saluted him, and pennons flapped out on a breeze like liquid silver, beneath a golden morning like the first morning of the world, and young Sir Galwyn's charger marched slow and stately with pride, and young Sir Galwyn looked not back whence he had come.

In a while they came to a forest. This was a certain enchanted forest and the trees in this forest were more ancient than any could remember; for it was beneath these trees that, in the olden time, one Sir Morvidus, Earl Warwick, had slain a giant which had assaulted Sir Morvidus with the trunk of a tree torn bodily from the earth; and Sir Morvidus to commemorate this encounter assumed the ragged staff for the cognizance which his descendants still bear. The trees of this forest were not as ordinary trees, for each bough bore a living eye and these eyes stared without winking at young Sir Galwyn as he rode beneath them. These boughs were never still, but writhed always as though in agony, and where one bough touched another they made desolate moaning. But young Sir Galwyn minded them not. His bright smooth face whereon naught was as yet written, shone serene beneath his plumed morion, and his beautiful blank shield whereon naught was as yet written, swung flashing from his saddlebow, while his stainless long sword made a martial clashing against his greaves and his golden spurs like twin lightnings. And Hunger and Pain rode always at his right hand and his left hand, and his shadow circled tireless before and beneath and behind him.

For seven days they rode through this forest where enchantments were as thick as mayflowers, and as they rode young Sir Galwyn conversed with Pain and Hunger, and because he was young he gained from them much information but no wisdom. On the seventh day, having pursued and slain a small dragon of an inferior and cowardly type which had evidently strayed prematurely from its den (so that this encounter is scarcely worth recording—indeed, as Hunger later reminded him, he had much better have slain a fallow deer) young Sir Galwyn and his two companions came upon a small ivycovered stone dwelling, upon the door of which young Sir Galwyn thundered stoutly with his axe helve. One appeared in reply to this summons and stood regarding young Sir Galwyn contemplatively, tickling its nose with a feather, and sneezing at intervals.

"Give you god-den, young master," said this one civilly.

Now this was civil enough, and sensible; but young Sir Galwyn was young and hasty, and being somewhat new at the trade of errantry and having expected a giant, or at least a dragon to answer his summons, knew not exactly what was expected of him here, the regulations of knighthood having no formula covering such a situation. Whereupon young Sir Galwyn, in righteous displeasure and with admirable presence of mind, thundered in return:

"What, varlet? what, minion! Would'st address a belted knight as young master? Hast no manners, knave?"

"Why now, as for that," replies the other gravely, "during all the years I have served the people it has ever been my policy to address all men as they would be addressed, king and cook, poet and hind. But, sir belted knight, before craving pardon of you I wish to remind you that we philosophers who, so to speak, live lives of retirement, cannot be expected to keep abreast of the latest quirks and fantasies of fashion regarding the approach by a stranger of a private dwelling and so forth; an we both be but as the other judge him, then by 'r lady, there are two of us here without manners."

"Ah, yes: you refer to these two staring gentlemen riding beside me. But they are friends: I vouch for them both."

"Ay, I know them," replied the other, smiling a little, "I have seen both these gaudy staring gentlemen before. In fact, but for them no one would ever ride into this enchanted wood."

Young Sir Galwyn looked doubtful and a trifle bewildered at this, then his stainless long sword clashed against his greaves and reminded him that he was Sir Galwyn. So young Sir Galwyn said:

"But enough of this: we are wasting time."

"On the contrary," rejoins the other courteously, "I assure you that you are causing me no inconvenience whatever. In fact, and I do not say it to flatter you, I find our conversation most salutary."

"I am afraid, friend," says young Sir Galwyn haughtily, "that I do not follow you."

"Why, you just remarked that you were wasting time, and I do assure you that I am suffering no inconvenience whatever from this rencontre."

Then says young Sir Galwyn: "There is something wrong here: one of the two of us is laboring under a delusion. I have been led by those who should know to believe that Time is an old gentleman with a long white beard; and now you who are not old and who certainly have no long white beard, set yourself up to be Time. How can this be?"

"Well," replies the other, "as for my personal appearance: in this enlightened day when, as any standard magazine will inform you, one's appearance depends purely on one's inclination or disinclination to change it, what reason could I possibly have for wishing to look older than I feel? Then my wife (who, I am desolated to inform you, is away for the weekend, visiting her parents) my wife thinks that it does not look well for a man in my business to resemble a doddering centenarian, particularly as my new system of doing business eliminates the middle man from all dealings with my customers."

"Ah," says young Sir Galwyn, "you also have reorganized your business then? This was done recently?"

"Fairly so," agrees the other. "Yesterday it was. Though translated into your temporal currency it boils up into quite an imposing mess. Let me see—something like two million years, though I cannot give the exact date off hand."

"Oh . . . ." Young Sir Galwyn ponders briefly while Pain and Hunger sat their steeds sedately on his right hand and his left hand. Then young Sir Galwyn says: "Certainly this is spoken glibly enough, but how can I know that you are really Time?"

The other shrugged. "You materialists! You are like crows, with a single cry for all occasions: 'Proof! Proof!' Well, then; take for example the proverb Time and tide wait for no man. Do you believe in the soundness of this proverb?"

"Surely: I have demonstrated this truth to my complete satisfaction. And it seems to me that you who, by your own account, have spent your life serving mankind in this wood, convict yourself."

"Very well. Let us begin by asking these two gentlemen who have ridden with you for some time and who should know, what you are." He turned to young Sir Galwyn's two companions and said: "Sir Green Design and Sir Red Design, what is this thing calling itself Sir Galwyn of Arthgyl?"

Whereupon the green design called Hunger and the red design called Pain answered together: "He is but a handful of damp clay which we draw hither and yon at will until the moisture is gone completely out of him, as two adverse winds toy with a feather; and when the moisture is all gone out of him he will be as any other pinch of dust, and we will not be concerned with him any longer."

"Why, really," says young Sir Galwyn, somewhat taken aback, "I had no idea that two travellers with whom one has shared hunger and hardship could have such an uncomplimentary opinion of one, let alone expressing it in such a bald manner. But, heigh ho, gentlemen! I see that I am but wasting my youth talking with two shadows and a doddering fool who would convince me that I am not even a shadow—a thing which I, who am Sir Galwyn of Arthgyl, know to be false just as I know that beyond the boundaries of this enchanted wood Fame awaits me with a little pain and some bloodshed, and at last much pleasure. For there I shall find and deliver from captivity a young princess whom I have seen in a dream and who reminds me of young hyacinths in spring. And which of you, who are two shadows and a doddering imbecile, can know or tell me differently?"

The green design which was called Hunger and the red design called Pain sat quietly in the intermittent shadows of young leaves, but the other

This illustration appears opposite page 3 of
Faulkner's text (page 47 in the present edition).

This illustration appears opposite page 38 of
Faulkner's text (page 82 in the present edition).

And the tale tells how at last one came to him. Dawn had already come without, flushing up the high small window so that this high small window which had been throughout the night only a frame for glow and scornful stars became now as a rose unfolding on the dark wall of the chapel. The song of birds came up on the dawn, and the young spring waking freshly, golden and white and troubling: flowers were birdcries about meadows unseen and birdcries were flowers neck-laced about the trees. Then the sun like a sword-blade touched his own stainless long sword, his morion and harberk and greaves, and his spurs like twin golden lightnings where they rested beneath the calm sorrowful gaze of the Young Compassionate One, touching his own young face where he had knelt all night on a stone floor, waiting for day.

And it was as though he had passed through a valley between shelving vague hills where the air was gray and smelled of spring, and had come at last upon a dark hurrying stream which, as he watched, became filled suddenly with atoms

3

Reproduction of page 3 (the first text page) of Faulkner's handlettered book.

raised his sad dark eyes and gazed upon young Sir Galwyn's bright empty face with envious admiration. "Ah, Sir Galwyn, Sir Galwyn," said this one, "what would I not give to be also young and heedless, yet with your sublime faith in your ability to control that destiny which some invisible and rather unimaginative practical joker has devised for you! Ah, but I too would then find this mad world an uncomplex place of light and shadow and good earth on which to disport me. Still, everyone to his taste. And certainly the taking of prodigious pains to overtake a fate which it is already written will inevitably find me, is not mine. So there is naught left but for each to follow that path which seems—no, not good: rather let us say, less evil—to him; and I who am immortal find it in my heart to envy you who are mortal and who inherited with the doubtful privilege of breathing a legacy of pain and sorrow and, at last, oblivion. Therefore, young Sir Galwyn of Arthgyl, in what way can I serve you?"

"Why, in what way save by directing me to the castle where a certain princess whose hair is like a column of fair sunny water is held captive?"

"Now your description, I am sure, is most comprehensive, and it is impossible that it fit any other princess than she who reminds you, as you have previously told me, of young hyacinths in spring. But has it not occurred to you that every young knight who rides into this enchanted wood seeks a maiden whose hair is like bright water and who reminds him of young hyacinths, or perhaps of narcissi, or of cherry bloom? So I repeat, though your description of her is most happily conceived, I must ask you to bear in mind the fact that I am an old man and that it has been many a day since a girl has clung in my heart as unforgettable as a branch of apple bloom (though my wife, I do assure you, is a matchless woman and I would not for the world have it thought that I do not appreciate her) so I fear it will be necessary for me to have something a bit more tangible than an emotional reaction to understand just what captive princess you refer to."

"Is this particular wood," says young Sir Galwyn, "so full of captive princesses that you cannot tell me which one I seek?"

"Now I do not intimate that every turret you are likely to see contains a sighing virgin playing the lute and languishing for deliverance and honorable wedlock; but certainly there are enough of them whose rank and beauty will please the most exacting taste. For instance, to the westward, not far from where the sun lies down at evening there languishes in a castle of green stone the Princess Elys, daughter of Sethynnen ap Seydnn Seidi called the Drunkard, King of Wales, and her shining sleek head is the evening star in the sky above the sunset. Or to the eastward, where the sun rises from the yellow morning, there languishes in a castle of yellow stone the Princess Aelia daughter of Aelian, prince among the Merovingians and Crown Marshall of Arles, and her shining sleek head is the morning star above the dawn. Now which of these two ladies most appeals to you? You cannot go wrong (though 'tis said the Princess Elys is rather given to tears and that the Princess Aelia being of a—well, lively disposition, left some talk behind her in Provence, not all of which was flattering. In fact, one hears that old Aelian himself had more to do with his daughter's deplorable capture than people generally know. But that is all as may be: is beside the point) Which ever one you choose, these two princes are well able to set a son-in-law up in any business he wishes."

"Ah, I do not know," says young Sir Galwyn. "How can I know which of these maidens is her whom I saw in a dream? Who is there who can tell me, since you admit that you cannot? Though I am sorry that these two princesses should pine in captivity, I cannot spend my youth chasing here and there, releasing captive maidens who for all I know are much happier in durance than they would be freed again and who might object to my meddling, for I must seek her who reminds me of honey and sunlight; and so—" young Sir Galwyn turns politely to the green design called Hunger and the red design called Pain "—and so, if you gentlemen are ready, we had better take leave of this puzzling incomprehensible stranger and get onward."

And the tale tells how young Sir Galwyn of Arthgyl rode on through this enchanted forest with Hunger at his right hand and Pain at his left hand while the hermit stood staring after young Sir Galwyn's retreating back with envious admiration. Then he shook his head and turned, and entered his hut again.

The border of the wood broke suddenly before him as a wave breaks, shattering into a froth of sunlight. Beyond him, up to the horizon and beyond it until his eyes felt like two falcons straining in their sockets, down and heath flowed in a long swooping flight to a rumourous blue haze. This was the sea.

A river cut the center of this plain, and young Sir Galwyn bore toward it. The stream was hidden beyond twinkling aspen and alder, and slender white birches like poised dancing girls; and one with a spear rose from the path, saying "Halt!"

Young Sir Galwyn regarded this green jerkined yeoman haughtily. "Stand aside, knave, and let me pass."

But the man-at-arms held his ground. "In the King's name, Lord, stop ye; else I must thrust my spear into this goodly steed, for none must pass hither on pain of my life."

"In the name of what king do you cry halt to a traveller on the public road, and to a belted knight at that? Stand aside: dost think to provoke my stainless long sword against thy scurvy carcase?"

"In the name of my master, Mark, King of Cornwall, do I bid all travellers halt at this point, for in yonder stream the princess Yseult is bathing; and no man, be he knight or varlet, may look upon the naked body of the bride of a king."

"Now, certainly," says young Sir Galwyn, "this is most strange. Who is your master, that he sends his bride gallivanting about the country, bathing in rivers, in charge of a man-at-arms?"

"It is not I who am in charge of this princess: it is King Mark's nephew, Tristram, whom you will find (were I to let you pass) lying in yonder shade and writhing with love for the maiden whom he has sworn a knightly oath to bring untarnished to the bed of his uncle. And it is my opinion that the sooner this maiden is delivered to King Mark the better for us all, for I do not like the look of this expedition. I am a family man and must take care of the appearance of things."

So young Sir Galwyn, without a backward glance at that thing which had been a Cornish man-at-arms, rode on down a shaded path toward a muted rumourous flashing of hidden water. One clad in armour rose and barred his way. "Halt, or die!" spoke this one in a terrible voice.

"Who bids Sir Galwyn of Arthgyl to halt?" rejoins young Sir Galwyn in cold displeasure, as they paused eyeing each other like two young wolf hounds. They were so much alike, from their bright young faces (though to be sure the other's face was not empty, being terrible with jealousy and passion)

64

to their mailed feet, that it was not strange that they should hate each other on sight.

"It is Tristram of Lyonness, by the grace of God and Uther Pendragon, knight; and he who would dispute this passage will be unshriven carrion beneath this sunset."

Now certainly, thinks young Sir Galwyn, I shall waste no time arguing with this unmannerly brute whose face is the color of thunder. And a would-be adulterer, also! Faith, and his vow of knighthood rests but lightly upon him who would make a Menelaus of his own uncle. But minstrels do sing of this Yseult, telling that she is as the morning star, and before her unguarded bosom's rich surprise men are maddened and their faces grow sharp as the spears of an assault. I am inclined to think it would be the part of wisdom to see this paragon of a maid while I have the opportunity, if only to tell my grandchildren of it in the years. "Ho, friend," he spake, "cannot one draw near enough to look upon this ward of thine?"

Without a word the other drew his sword and furiously attacked young Sir Galwyn, so young Sir Galwyn slew this one, and tethered his horse to a near-by tree. At the end of the glade was a screen of willow and aspen; beyond this screen, young Sir Galwyn knew, would be water. So young Sir Galwyn drew near and parted the slender willows and the tire- and waiting-women of the Princess Yseult scurried with shrill cries, like plump partridges. And the Princess Yseult, who stood like a young birch tree in the water, screamed delicately, putting her two hands before her eyes.

"Ah, Tristram, Tristram!" says she, "wouldst violate thine own uncle's bed? Mother Mary, protect me from this ravisher!" then spreading her fingers a little more: "Why, this is not Sir Tristram! Who is this strange young man who dares approach the bride of a king in her bath? Help, wenches: protect me!"

"No, lady," replies young Sir Galwyn, "I am Galwyn of Arthgyl, knight at the hand of the Constable du Boisgeclin, who, having heard the beauty of the Princess Yseult sung by many a minstrel in many a banquetting hall, must needs dare all things to see her; and who, now that he has gazed upon her, finds that all his life before this moment was a stale thing, and that all the beautiful faces upon which he has looked are as leaves in a wind; and that you who

66

are like honey and sunlight and young hyacinths have robbed him of peace and contentment as a gale strips the leaves from a tree; and because you are the promised bride of a king there is no help for it anywhere."

Well, really, thinks the princess on hearing these words, such a nice-spoken young man would hardly have the courage to harm anyone . . . . . I am afraid. Then aloud: "Who are you, and how have you managed to pass Sir Tristram, who swore that none should draw near?"

"Ah, lady," rejoins young Sir Galwyn, "what boots it who I am, who have now found all beauty and despair and all delight in an inaccessible place to which living I can never attain and which dead I can never forget? As for your Sir Tristram of Lyonness: I do not know him, unless he be one I have recently slain in yonder glade."

"Do you really think I am beautiful?" says the Princess Yseult in pleased surprise, "You say it so convincingly that I must believe you have said it before—I am sure you have said that to other girls. Now, haven't you? But I am sorry you saw me with my hair done this way. It does not suit me at all . . . . . So you have killed that impossible Sir Tristram.

Really I am not at all sorry: I have stood in this cold water until, as you can see—" blushing delightfully "—that my skin is completely covered with goose bumps, and I made that stupid young man promise three times that none should approach me. It is a shame that one as handsome as he should be so impossibly dull . . . . . . I am distressed you should have seen me with my hair done like this, but then you know what maids are in these degenerate days."

And the tale tells how the Princess Yseult came naked out of the water and she and young Sir Galwyn sojourned in the shade of a tree discussing various things, and how young Sir Galwyn's glib tongue wove such a magic that the Princess Yseult purred like a kitten. And afterwards they talked some more and the Princess Yseult told young Sir Galwyn all about herself and Sir Tristram and King Mark, and so forth and so on. But after a while young Sir Galwyn began to be restlessly aware that young hyacinths were no longer fresh, once you had picked them. So breaking into the middle of the plans the Princess Yseult was comfortably making for hers and young Sir Galwyn's future, young Sir Galwyn said:

"Lady, though the sound of your voice is as that of lute strings touched sweetly among tapers in a

windless dusk and therefore I will never tire of hearing it, and though your body is as a narrow pool of
fair water in this twilight, do you not think—" diffi-
dently "—that it would be wise to call your women
and put something on it beside the green veils of this
twilight? You know how difficult a spring cold can
be."

"Why, how thoughtful of you, Galwyn!
But, really now, there is no hurry, is there? Surely
we cannot go anywhere this late. But then, perhaps
you are right about my getting into some clothes:
someone might drop in. I blush to think of it, but for
some reason—though it is not at all like myself—I
feel no sense of immodesty whatever in being naked
with you, for you are different from other men: you
really understand me. However, perhaps you are
right. Do you wait here quietly for me: I shall not be
long. Now, promise not to follow me, not to move."

So young Sir Galwyn promised and the
Princess Yseult kissed him and closed his eyes with
her finger tips and kissed his eyelids and made him
promise not to open them until she was out of sight,
and retired. Young Sir Galwyn was too much of a
gentleman to open them or to tell the Princess Yseult
that he preferred seeing her back to her front, naked

or otherwise, so he sat until the Princess Yseult had had ample time to collect her women, whereupon young Sir Galwyn rose and with furtive nonchalance betook him to the tree where his horse was tethered, and where the green design called Hunger and the red design called Pain waited him courteously; and they mounted and rode away from that place. And young Sir Galwyn at last drew a deep breath.

"By my faith, sir," spoke Hunger, "that was surely no sigh of a lover reft recently of his mistress? It struck me as being rather more a sigh of relief."

"To be frank with you, friend, I do not know myself exactly what that exhalation signified. Surely, one cannot find in this world one fairer than her whom I have recently left, and it seemed to me that all life must halt while I gazed upon her body like a young birch tree in the dusk, or felt the texture of her hair like a column of sunny water; still . . . . . "

"—still, this maid who is fairer than a man may hope to find more than once in a lifetime, must fain interpose between you that less fair but more tireless virtue which lives behind her little white teeth," the green design called Hunger completed for him.

"Exactly. And I now know that she is no

different from all the other girls I have known, be they plain or be they beautiful. It occurs to me," young Sir Galwyn continued profoundly, that it is not the thing itself that man wants, so much as the wanting of it. But ah, it is sharper than swords to know that she who is fairer than music could not content me for even a day."

"But that, Sir Galwyn, is what life is: a ceaseless fretting to gain shadows to which there is no substance. To my notion man is a buzzing fly blundering through a strange world, seeking something he can neither name nor recognize and probably will not want. Still, you are young and you have a certain number of years to get through some how, so better luck next time."

So they rode on beneath squadrons of high pale stars, westward where the sky was like transparent oiled green silk upon a full and glowing breast, and a single star like a silver rose pinned to it. There was a faint greenish glow about them, and fireflies were like blown sparks from invisible fires. Suddenly a milk white doe bounded into the glade before them and kneeling before young Sir Galwyn, begged him to pierce her with his sword. Young Sir

Galwyn did so, and lo! there knelt before him Elys, daughter of the King of Wales. She wore a green robe and a silver girdle studded with sapphires and she took young Sir Galwyn by the hand and led him deeper into the forest to a tent of lilac colored silk and ivory poles, and a bed of rushes. And young Sir Galwyn looked into the west and he saw that the evening star was no longer there.

And the tale tells how after a while young Sir Galwyn waked and raised himself to his elbow. The Princess Elys yet slept and young Sir Galwyn looked upon her in a vague sadness, and he kissed her sleeping mouth with a feeling of pity for her and of no particular pride in himself, and he rose quietly and passed without the tent. So he mounted his horse again.

The east was becoming light: high above him the morning star swam immaculately in a river of space. He heard faint horns triumphant as flung banners, and the horns grew louder. Then all at once he was surrounded by heralds with trumpets, and sarabands of dancing girls circled about him: their breasts were stained with gold and lipped with vermilion, and pages in scarlet lept among them. Then came a chariot of gold with a canopy of amythest on scarlet poles; nine white dolphins drew the chariot and in the chariot was the Princess Aelia, daughter of Aelius the Merovingian, dressed in a yellow robe and a girdle of sapphires, and the Princess Aelia stopped and leaned toward him.

"Come, Sir Galwyn of Arthgyl. I have long awaited you."

"Ah, lady," says young Sir Galwyn, "I am as one who has thirsted in a desert, and who sees before him in a dream a region of all beauty and despair and of all delight."

The Princess Aelia was pleased at this. "What a charming speech! I have heard of you, Sir Galwyn, but I had not thought to find such a nice spoken young man, or one so handsome. So come, and please to enter my chariot, and let us be going."

So young Sir Galwyn entered, and the trumpets flourished, and the nine white dolphins which drew the chariot moved like the wind. And looking upward young Sir Galwyn saw that the morning star was gone.

"Now then," says the Princess Aelia, "we can talk comfortably. So tell me about yourself."

"What can he tell you, Princess," replies young Sir Galwyn, "who has sought the whole earth over for one he has seen in a dream, who reminds him of honey and sunlight and young hyacinths; and who at last finds her in the person of an immortal whom he may only cry after as an infant in darkness, and whom he dare not touch? And because she is fairer than the song of birds at dawn or the feet of the Loves that make light in the air like doves' wings, he may never get her out of his heart, and because she is an immortal and a princess, there is no help for it any-where."

"Why, do you really think that I am beauti-ful?" says the Princess Aelia in pleased surprise. "I am sorry you saw me in this rag. I hate yellow: it makes me look—oh—fat, and I am not fat. But you say that rather glibly—" giving him a glance of bright suspicion "—how many girls have you told that to, Sir Galwyn?"

"Well," says young Sir Galwyn, slightly ill at ease, "there was a certain Yseult, going to wed with the King of Cornwall, whom I paused out of curiosity to watch bathing in a pool and who insisted on my stopping to talk with her (which I could not refuse out of sheer politeness) I think I said some-thing of this nature to her; and there was the Princess Elys who stopped me in a forest and who insisted that I accompany her to her tent to pass the night, and this too politeness forbade my refusing. And I may have said something like this to her."

"If that isn't just like a man!" exclaimed the Princess Aelia incomprehensibly. Then she stared at young Sir Galwyn with curiosity and some respect. "But I really must say, you are certainly a fast worker, as well as a discreet young man . . . . the Princess Elys! that yellow haired hussy! Heavens, what abysmal taste! Oh, men are such children: any toy for the moment. Really, I cannot see how you could have the nerve to repeat to me the same speeches you have made to a girl who roams forests at night and accosts strange young men. She is very evidently no better than she should be." The Princess Aelia stared away into space for a while. The chariot had left earth far behind and was now rushing through the sky, crashing through silver clouds like a swift ship among breakers, while falcons on planing rigid wings and with eyes like red and yellow jewels whirled about it, screaming.

The Princess Aelia continued: "To leave a creature like that, and come to me! With the same words on your lips! Ah, you have no respect for me," she wailed, "associating my name with a creature like that!" She burst into tears. "No, no, dont try to justify yourself! To think that I have come off alone with a man like you! What will my good name be worth now? How can I hold my head up ever again? Oh, I hate you, I hate you!"

"Now certainly, lady," says young Sir Galwyn, "you cannot blame me for this situation: it was on your invitation that I first entered this golden chariot."

This was sound logic, and had its usual result. "Dont talk to me!" wept the Princess Aelia, "it is just as I expected from a man like you: to injure me irreparably, and then try to justify yourself in my eyes."

"Well, this may be remedied by taking me back to earth. I am sure that I had no intention of doing anyone an injury. In fact, I cannot see that I have accomplished any hurt to you."

"But how can taking you back to earth remedy things? You will sit around low taverns and simply tear my reputation to shreds. Oh, I know you men! What am I to do?"

"Then," says young Sir Galwyn, "if you wont take me back to earth, I'll go back alone." And young Sir Galwyn threw his leg over the side of the chariot.

The Princess Aelia shrieked and threw her arms about him. "No, no! you'll be killed!"

"Then will you promise to stop crying and blaming me for something I have not done?"

"Yes." So young Sir Galwyn drew in his leg and the Princess Aelia dried her eyes on her sleeve. "Really, Galwyn, you are too stupid for words. But it did hurt me to find that, after all the nice things you said to me, or led me to believe, that I am no more to you than that—" and the Princess Aelia used a shocking word.

Young Sir Galwyn was properly shocked. "Really, Princess, I must object to such terms being applied to my friends. Besides, a lady would never know such a word, let alone repeat it."

"Oh, your ladies and your friends! Pooh, what do I care for either? But, tell me truly," clinging to him, "dont you think I am better looking than she?"

"Why, now," begins young Sir Galwyn lamely.

"Oh, you brute, I hate you! Why did I ever

come away with such a beast! I wish I were dead!"

"Yes, yes!" young Sir Galwyn almost shouted, "anything if you wont cry again!"

"Ah, Galwyn, Galwyn, why are you so abysmally truthful? If you knew anything about women, you'd have learned better. But how can you have learned anything about women, poor dear, having been so successful with them? Anyway, you shouldn't have taken up with that nasty little Elys. But I'll show you what love is, Sir Galwyn; ah, I'll show you something you'll not soon forget!"

She spoke to the nine white dolphins in a strange tongue, and they turned earthward and flew at a dizzying speed. Young Sir Galwyn would have screamed with fear but the Princess Aelia's mouth was on his and young Sir Galwyn could not scream; and time and eternity swirled up and vortexed about the rush of their falling and the earth was but a spinning bit of dust in a maelstrom of blue space. The falcons planed plummetting beside the chariot and the wind screamed through the feathers of their wings, and the red and yellow jewels of their eyes were like coals of fire fanned to a heat unbearable. Young Sir Galwyn was no longer afraid: never had his heart known such ecstasy! he was a god and a falling star, consuming the whole world in a single long swooping rush through measureless regions of horror and delight down down, leaving behind him no change of light nor any sound.

A nd the tale tells how, in a while, young Sir Galwyn waked in a forest. Near him was his tethered steed browsing on the tender leaves of a young poplar, and beside it on two more horses sat the green design that was called Hunger and the red design called Pain, gravely and sedately waiting. So young Sir Galwyn rose and mounted, and the three of them rode away from that place. And young Sir Galwyn drew a deep breath.

"By my faith, sir," quoth Hunger, "that was surely no sigh of a lover reft recently of his mistress? It struck me as being rather more a sigh of relief."

"To be frank with you, friend, I do not myself know exactly what that exhalation signified. Surely, a man is not to find in this world three fairer ladies than I have found in as many days; and yet . . . ."

"Ay, Sir Galwyn, and yet and yet. You have known the bride of a king before ever her husband looked upon her, you have possessed, in the persons

79

of the daughters of the two most important minor princes in Christendom, the morning and the evening stars, and yet you have gained nothing save a hunger which gives you no ease. I remember to have remarked once that man is a buzzing insect blundering through a strange world, seeking something he can neither name nor recognize, and probably will not want. I think now that I shall refine this aphorism to: Man is a buzzing fly beneath the inverted glass tumbler of his illusions." Hunger fell silent and the three of them paced steadily on amid the dappled intermittent shadows. Flowers were about the glades merrily, and birds sang every where, and the sun shone full on young Sir Galwyn's face on which was at last something written although it was not a thing of which young Sir Galwyn was especially proud, and his shield swung from his saddlebow and it did not flash quite as brightly as it once did, for there was something written on it also that young Sir Galwyn was not particularly proud of, and young Sir Galwyn's long sword had stained through its scabbard and so young Sir Galwyn drew the skirt of his cloak over his sword

Hunger spoke again in a while: "There is still one more girl I may show you, and I guarantee that she will smoothe that look of hunger from your face. What say you, young Sir Galwyn? Shall we seek this maid?"

And young Sir Galwyn said: "Who is this maid who can smoothe all hunger and remembering from my face?"

And the other replied: "It is my sister."

And young Sir Galwyn said: "Lead on."

So the three of them rode onward into the west from which the last light was ebbing as from a smooth beach.

This place, too, was familiar. That is, it seemed to young Sir Galwyn that soon there would appear something that he had seen and known long since, that here would be reenacted a scene that he had once looked upon or taken part in. So they rode on through a valley between shelving vague hills where the air was gray and smelled of spring. At last, at young Sir Galwyn's feet lay a dark hurrying stream and beside the stream stood a tree covered with leaves of a thousand different colors, and near the tree was a paunchy little man neither standing nor lying, with a beautiful white high brow and eyes of no particular color, resembling nothing so much as water wherein a great many things had been drowned. And young Sir Galwyn stopped at the brink of the stream and Hunger and Pain paused obediently near him, and as he gazed into the dark hurrying waters he knew that he had stood here before, and he wondered if his restless seeking through the world had been only a devious unnecessary way of returning to a place he need never have left.

In a while he of the calm beautiful brow drew near to young Sir Galwyn and he made a gesture with his long pale hand. Whereupon Hunger and Pain withdrew, and they were in a desolate place. And he with the high white brow said to young Sir Galwyn:

"Choose."

And young Sir Galwyn asked: "What shall I choose?"

But the other only replied: "Look, and see."

So they stood side by side, staring into the dark waters. And as they watched the waters were no longer dark but were filled with formless fragments of color and sound like darting small fish which, as young Sir Galwyn watched, began to coalesce into a regular measured succession of light and dark.

"Now," said the paunchy little man who looked as though standing up was very uncomfortable for him, "you, who have crossed this stream once without being wetted, must now choose one of two things. In this hurrying dark flood will appear the various phases of all life, from the beginning of time down to this moment, left in this stream by those who have preceded you here and whose memories have been washed clean and blank and smooth as a marble surface after rain. And now, having completed the cycle I have allowed you, you may choose any one of these phases to live over again. And though you will be but a shadow among shades it will seem to you that this which is now transpiring was but a dark dream which you had dreamed and that you are a palpable thing directing your destiny in a palpable world.

"Or you may choose to be submerged in these waters. Then you will remember nothing, not even this conversation or this choosing; and all your petty victories, your loving and hating, all the actions you have achieved will be washed from your mind to linger in these hurrying dark waters like darting small fish for those who are to come here after you to gaze upon; and this is Fame. But once these waters have closed above you, your memory will be as a smooth surface after rain, and you will remember nothing at all."

"What, then," says young Sir Galwyn, "will I be?"

"You will not be anything."

"Not even a shadow?"

"Not even a shadow."

"And if I choose to cross this stream, how may I do so without being wetted?"

The other moved his pale smooth hand and there appeared from out the mist beyond the dark hurrying water a gray man in a gray boat without oars. The boat touched the shore at their feet and the gray man stood with his head bent, staring into the water, and his gray garment hung from his lean figure in formal motionless folds.

"And if I choose to cross this stream?" repeated young Sir Galwyn.

"As I have already told you, you will be a shadow subject to all shadowy ills—hunger and pain and bodily discomforts, and love and hate and hope and despair. And you will know no better how to combat them than you did on your last journey through the world, for my emigration laws prohibit Experience leaving my domains. And besides, man should beware of Experience as he should beware of all women, for with her or without her he will be miserable, but without her he will not be danger-ous."

"Then I will no longer be that thing men call Sir Galwyn of Arthgyl?"

"You will no longer be that thing men call Sir Galwyn of Arthgyl."

"But, if I am a shadow, how can I know hunger and pain?"

The other raised his head. His eyes were the color of sleep and he regarded young Sir Galwyn wearily. "Have not Hunger and Pain been beside you since before you could remember? have they not ridden at your right hand and your left hand in all your journeys and battles? were they not closer to you than the young Yseult and Elys and Aelia could ever attain, or any of them who reminded you of honey and sunlight and young hyacinths in spring?"

"Yes, that is true . . . ." young Sir Galwyn admitted slowly. "But," he said suddenly, "I was not a shadow then."

"How do you know you were not a shadow?"

Young Sir Galwyn thought a while, and it was as though a cold wind had blown upon him. Then he said: "Who are you, who bids me choose one of two alternatives, neither of which is particularly pleasing to me?"

"I am the Lord of Sleep."

And young Sir Galwyn regarded the paunchy little man with the beautiful high brow and eyes the color of sleep, and young Sir Galwyn was silent. In a while the other said:

"Look."

And young Sir Galwyn looked as he was bid, and in the hurrying dark waters were three faces. The Princess Yseult, now Queen of Cornwall, returned his gaze, haughty with power and offended pride, and passed on; the face of the Princess Elys, daughter of the King of Wales, whom he had abandoned in the enchanted forest looked at him in reproach and sorrow. Her face was blurred as with weeping, and she raised her delicate young arms to him as she sank away into the dark stream. The third was the glittering passionate face of Aelia, princess of the Merovingians; she gave him a fierce glance and her mouth was a thin red scorn and she too passed onward with the other glittering wreckage in the water, and Pain and Hunger drawing near again said together:

"Look."

And Hunger and Pain drew subtly nearer, and there in the water was one all young and white, and with long shining hair like a column of fair sunny water, and young Sir Galwyn thought of young hyacinths in spring, and honey and sunlight. Young Sir Galwyn looked upon this face and he was as one sinking from a fever into a soft and bottomless sleep; and he stepped forward into the water and Hunger and Pain went away from him, and as the water touched him it seemed to him that he knelt in a dark room waiting for day and that one like a quiet soft shining came to him, saying: "Rise, Sir Galwyn; be faithful, fortunate, and brave."

And the tree covered with leaves of a thousand different colours spoke, and all the leaves whirled up into the air and spun about it; and the tree was an old man with a shining white beard like a silver cuirass, and the leaves were birds.

What sayest thou, good Saint Francis?

"Little sister Death," said the good Saint Francis.

Thus it was in the old days.

And young Sir Galwyn regarded the paunchy little man with the beautiful high brow and eyes the color of sleep, and young Sir Galwyn was silent. In a while the other said:

"Look."

And young Sir Galwyn looked as he was bid, and in the hurrying dark waters were three faces. The Princess Yseult, now Queen of Cornwall, returned his gaze, haughty with power and offended pride, and passed on; the face of the Princess Elys, daughter of the King of Wales, whom he had abandoned in the enchanted forest looked at him in reproach and sorrow. Her face was blurred as with weeping, and she raised her delicate young arms to him as she sank away into the dark stream. The third was the glittering passionate face of Aelia, princess of the Merovingians; she gave him a fierce glance and her mouth was a thin red scorn and she too passed onward with the other glittering wreckage in the water, and Pain and Hunger drawing near again said together:

"Look."

And Hunger and Pain drew subtly nearer, and there in the water was one all young and white, and with long

42

This illustration appears opposite page 18 of
Faulkner's text (page 62 in the present edition).